Jemima and the
Welsh Rabbit

Jemima and the Welsh Rabbit

GILLIAN AVERY

Illustrated by
JOHN LAWRENCE

HAMISH HAMILTON

First published in Great Britain 1972 by
Hamish Hamilton Children's Books Ltd
90 Great Russell Street, London WC1B 3PT

Reprinted 1974
SBN 241 02227 4

Printed in Great Britain by
Lewis Reprints Ltd.
member of Brown, Knight & Truscott Group
London and Tonbridge

Reindeer Books

Chapter 1

A HUNDRED YEARS ago there were many more railways all over England. There were not only main lines between the big cities, but scores of little lines that branched off them and served small villages and market towns. The railways all belonged to separate companies who dressed up their trains in their own particular colours and competed against each other to produce the fastest service, the smartest trains, and the greatest comfort for their passengers.

The town where Jemima Judkin lived in 1870 was near the border of England and Wales, and it was served by two railways, which I shall call the Grand Union Railway and the Hereford and Shropshire Railway. The Grand Union had beautiful trains, bright blue picked out with orange and black lines, and their engines were called by the names of

castles and kings. But the Hereford and Shropshire engines were only dirty green and were
mostly given girls' names and rather silly ones
at that, like Lizzy and Mabel.

There were two railways, and two stations,
and Jemima Judkin lived in the part of the
town that lay between them. It was rather a
dreary area of narrow streets and smoke-
grimed little houses. All day long and far into

the night the engines whistled and screamed, and the trucks in the goods yards and the sidings clanged and rattled as they were shunted. Most of the children who lived there had fathers who worked on one or other of the railways, and they all of course supported the railway that their particular father belonged to. The Grand Union children (who called themselves the Grands) in some ways had the best of it, because the Grand Union railway was one of the crack lines of England, with the fastest trains and smartest engines, whereas the Hereford and Shropshire was known as the Halt and Sleep because it was so slow.

But the Halt and Sleep children (whom their opponents called the Sleepers) had Jemima Judkin to lead them, and she really was a force to be reckoned with. She had a mop of frizzy black hair on which no hat would ever sit straight, and shining red cheeks that were so bright that once a teacher who didn't know her had sent her home from school saying that the child had scarlet fever.

She loved battles. In next to no time she could whistle up a horde of supporters and set them on to her enemies. Very bold Grands might put their heads round the street corner and yell

Jemima's pa don't go far.
He can only creep on the Halt and Sleep.

But they had to be very bold and very fleet-footed because in a matter of seconds Jemima would have a throng of Sleepers after them, and she herself could do terrible damage with her slate, which she would smash down with both hands on the heads of her enemies. After an encounter like that it was nearly always the Grands who crawled away to lick their wounds and mutter vengeance against Jemima Judkin.

But Jemima, while she gloried in her victories, did often wish that it was the Grands she was leading, and that her father belonged to a railway company that was worthy of her.

She was in a mood like this that hot summer day in 1870 when she trudged home from school. The Sleepers had taunted the Grands in the playground about a train that had run off the rails, and the Grands had pointed out that at least their trains *ran*, they didn't limp like gammy-legged tortoises. Then all the Grands started shouting "gammy-legged tortoises" at Jemima and her followers. It was then that Jemima discovered—not having a slate to hand—what a good weapon her head

was. She butted the Grand leader in his chest and he went down like an ox in front of the butcher. Then she went for his followers. None of them had realised how hard a head could be, and they soon retreated howling, far too soon for Jemima. It had felt glorious while it lasted, like a bull charging. But now there was nothing left, except a very hot afternoon, and nothing in particular to do in it.

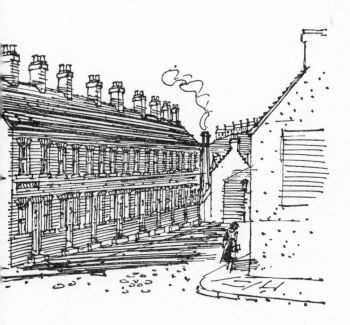

The Judkins lived in Paradise Terrace, which was not nearly such a nice place as it sounded, and Jemima's mother often lamented that she was not back living in the Herefordshire country where she had been brought up as a girl. The terrace was a long row of houses, all joined together, and all exactly alike. Each had a brown front door with a small window on either side of it and two more upstairs. There was no garden, of course, but the kitchen steps at the back led down to a tiny yard behind each house. The paint on the front door that day was almost too hot to touch, and you could have fried an egg on the door knocker. Jemima let it fall with a thundering whack which brought the neighbours on either side to peer through their lace curtains to see whatever was going on.

"Jemima Judkin," said her mother angrily as she opened the door, "what call have you got to be making a noise like that?"

"The knocker was hot," Jemima said crossly. "It nearly burnt my fingers off."

"And what a sight you are, fit to frighten the crows. No hat as usual. Sometimes I don't know how I can hold up my head for the shame of having you as a daughter. Have you been fighting again?"

"They called us gammy-legged tortoises," said Jemima defensively.

"And I know what's going to happen, we'll be having their fathers knocking at the door this evening and complaining about you and your carryings on. Not for the first time of course. Where are you going to now?"

"Out in the yard," said Jemima.

"You keep out of mischief then or it'll be the worse for you."

There was not much chance of mischief in the yard, which was empty except for a pot of stunted geraniums and a small patch of shade. But Jemima loafed down the kitchen steps in the hope that the next-door boys might be in their yard. They were Grands and could be taunted. They were also boys, and Jemima, though there were of course boys among her Sleepers, had a particular hatred for boys.

But the next-door yard was silent. All you could hear that burning July day was a fretful baby wailing somewhere at the end of the terrace, and of course the everlasting whistling and shrieking of trains in the nearby sidings. What a horrible place it was to live in, Jemima thought angrily.

Then there was the sound of a window being thrown up in the next house. Two heads leered down at her, two tongues were stuck out, and two voices started shouting:

> Oh JEE mima, look at your uncle Jim,
> He's in the peasoup learning how to swim.
> First he does the breast stroke, then he does the side,
> Now he's under the water, swimming against the tide!

Jemima had no uncle Jim, and she pretended to take no notice.

"Look at her sticking up her nose in the air!" shrieked the boys with delight. "Ain't you afraid a blackbird'll come along and peck it off?"

"You'll fall out of that window," said Jemima savagely.

"Oooh what a nasty mess there'll be then, as red as them flaming cheeks of yours!"

The heat and the boredom had made Jemima feel violent. She snatched up the pot of geraniums and flung it at the grinning faces. It was a beautiful shot. The faces withdrew in a flash and there was a gratifying smashing sound from inside the room.

"Our dad's just coming in," howled one of the boys. "You'll cop it now. He'll come and wallop you, just see if he don't."

Jemima knew he would, but it was worth it. She would have done the same again to hear that lovely crash. She went indoors to await events.

"Your pa's at the front door," called her mother from the kitchen. "Go and tell him tea's ready."

Mr Judkin and the next-door's dad were going to meet on the doorstep, and it was only a matter of seconds before trouble would come hurtling down on Jemima. She dragged her feet down the dark little passage and undid the door.

"And you get your young louts in order before you come complaining about my girl," she heard Mr Judkin saying. "As nasty a lot as any in the terrace, they are. I'm thankful we'll soon be shot of the pack of them."

This was not the way Jemima had expected her father to act. He slammed the door shut and gave her a smacking kiss—which again was unexpected.

"You go and tell your ma to see there's a real good tea. I'll be through as soon as I've had a bit of a sluice."

Jemima went into the kitchen. It was very hot in there because of the cooking range, and she could see it was not going to be a nice tea at all. The butter was an oily pool in the glass dish and the jam was plum which none of them liked. The pressed beef was greasy with

heat, and they were nearly at an end of the pickled onions and the madeira cake. From the little scullery across the passage came cheerful splashing noises and the sound of Mr Judkin singing.

"Your pa seems very up in his spirits," said Mrs Judkin. "Funny. I thought I heard him having words with that Mr Bloor."

"Pa slammed the door shut in Mr Bloor's face," said Jemima.

"There now! I won't be able to go into my own backyard because of what Mrs Bloor will have to say across the wall about *that*," lamented Mrs Judkin. "Paradise Terrace fair gets me down, at times, it really does."

Mr Judkin, his hair sleeked down with water, and smelling strongly of Monkey Brand soap, appeared at this moment. "You cock a snook at the Bloors—and all the terrace too! We'll soon be clear of *them*!"

"Whatever are you on about, Joe?" said Mrs Judkin faintly, sitting down with a flop.

"We're leaving Paradise Terrace for good, that's what I'm on about, Em my girl."

"You mean to say you've got another job?"

"From the end of July I'll be a station-master, and you'll be living in the country among the hills like what you've always wanted. So've I, for that matter. A strip of garden, a house where you can move your elbows without jabbing them into the neighbours' backyard, and green fields and good clean air—that's what I would like. I've had my stomachful of Paradise Terrace."

"Oh Joe, I never thought it could happen," said Mrs Judkin weakly, dabbing at her eyes with her apron. "Your own station *and* the country. Where is it?"

"A little place called Bredeworthy up near the Welsh hills. And the stationmaster's house is just down the lane from the station—snug little place it sounds."

"Is it Grand Union or H & S?" said Jemima sharply.

"It's neither. It's a private line off of High-church junction."

"What's it called then?" demanded Jemima.

"The Bredeworthy line, they call it."

"Who does it belong to?"

"There's some farmers who live up Bredeworthy way who wanted a railway to take
their milk and that to Highchurch, and they
had it built a few years back. And that's quite
enough from you. You hold your tongue
while your mother and me talk."

Of course Jemima would have liked it to be
a station on a line that her friends and her
enemies had heard of. But being Jemima she
held her head high and talked loftily to the
other children about having a father who was
a stationmaster. The boys next door changed
their song. Now they chanted

Oh JEE mima, look at your old dad.
He's on the platform a'waving of his
flag.
First he waves the red one, then he
waves the green.
But he needn't wave the red one if
Jemima's face is seen!

But Jemima didn't hurl any more geraniums

at them because she knew they were jealous really.

So on a hot day towards the end of the month, Jemima and Mrs Judkin turned the key on the empty house in Paradise Terrace and, laden with baskets and parcels, got into the fly that was to take them to the station. Mr Judkin had left much earlier on the cart that was taking all the furniture to their new home. A couple of neighbours looked at them through the lace curtains, but otherwise nobody seemed to notice, and the group of children—Grands *and* Sleepers—who were playing marbles together happily at the end of the street, did not even look up from their game. Jemima seemed to have gone right out of their lives already, as if she had never existed. The Grands and Sleepers had forgotten that they were supposed to be enemies. It was a sad moment.

Jemima and her mother arrived at High-church junction late in the afternoon, and Mrs Judkin, who had been in a state of nervous alarm throughout the journey in case they were on the wrong train, fell out of the carriage as if it had been red hot.

"Quickly, Jemima, find a porter, do, and ask him where the Bredeworthy train goes from. Quickly, it may be going this very minute."

But when Jemima did find a porter and breathlessly gasped out her question, he only laughed. "The *Welsh Rabbit*? No call to hurry for her. You sit down and enjoy the beautiful sunshine."

So Jemima and her mother sat there and sweltered, surrounded by their parcels. Trains came in at other platforms, people got off, doors banged, but there was never a sign of life on theirs. At last, when the shadows were growing long, a few people with market baskets straggled along, and the porter crossed over to their side and stood staring down the line, shading his eyes from the sun.

"There she be," he called, pointing to a feather of smoke far away round a curve. Only Mrs Judkin leapt to her feet; the other passengers sat on the bench and went on with their chattering and squawks of laughter.

Jemima had never seen such a comic figure of a train as drew up alongside their platform. It was far removed from the magnificent castles and kings of the Grand Union line, or from any of the locomotives of the Hereford and Shropshire, dirty green and slow though they might be. It was small and plump with a high funnel, and it drew behind it just one rather battered carriage and a guard's van. The engine's name was painted on its side, and a more ludicrous name Jemima had never met —the *Welsh Rabbit*. One very fat man and one small thin one peered down at Mrs Judkin and Jemima from the cab.

"You in any hurry?" said the fat man. "My mate's got a job for his missus in the town. The fact is," he added confidentially, "it's her legs that's took bad and he said he'd get her a bottle of something to rub on. Why, upon my word, now I know who you are. You're for Bredeworthy station and the station-master's house. What a bit of luck we was late enough leaving to see the cart coming down

the lane back there with all your traps on
board. You'll be glad to know Mr Judkin's
there safe and sound, I daresay. You climb
on, and my mate'll be the quickest he
can."

Even so, Jemima and her mother had to
wait for what seemed hours. The varnished
wood of the carriage seats felt red-hot, and a
crateful of hens on the floor near them kept
up a continuous outraged cackle. And the passengers kept up their cackle too, greeting
everybody by name as they climbed in, and
shouting remarks down the length of the carriage. None of them seemed in the least of a
hurry. Mrs Judkin was too tired to budge, but
Jemina from time to time thrust her head
furiously out of the window, only to find the
fat engine driver sitting on a milk churn on
the platform telling long, long stories to the
porter.

And even when the train did start it never
kept moving for more than a few minutes at
a time. It was forever stopping in places where
there were no stations at all, only fields, as

well as at wayside halts that were nothing but a platform and a name.

"Victor Williams's heifers, I daresay," said the owner of the hens after one such stop when Jemina had complained loudly. "There's no keeping them in when they've got a mind to jump that hedge. You get down

and help Mr Pugh get them back in the field.
No? Well, we're not far from Bredeworthy
now, and I reckon your poor Ma'll be more
than ready for her cup of tea."

"Us at Bredeworthy?" said Mrs Judkin, sitting up with a jerk. "Jemima, get them parcels
together quick. Put your hat straight, button
up your coat, and whatever you do, don't
leave anything behind."

But the hens' owner leaned forward and
gave Mrs Judkin a motherly pat on the knee.
"Don't you fret. It'll be a bit of time yet before
Mr Pugh gathers them heifers off the line. And
the *Welsh Rabbit* don't go no farther than
Bredeworthy. She'll be there till tomorrow
morning—that'll give you plenty of time. You
sit down and take it easy, like the rest of us."

Chapter 2

MRS JUDKIN need not have worried, for when the *Welsh Rabbit* drew up with a last decisive jolt at Bredeworthy station, Mr Judkin was waiting there to help her and Jemima with the parcels and baskets and to lead them down the lane to the house. While her parents gathered the packages together, Jemima looked about her. The station was tiny, just one platform with a small stone building on it, and a flowerbed with the word "Bredeworthy" picked out in shells. On the other side of the line was a big shed where she supposed the *Welsh Rabbit* was going to spend the night. And behind that were steep wooded hills. The railway went no farther; it ended in Bredeworthy. It was not much of a place for Jemima Judkin, the leader of the Sleepers, the arch-enemy of the Grands.

Mr Judkin took them through the little

white gate at the end of the platform and down a grassy lane.

"The old stationmaster is working till to-morrow, so I can take things a bit easy," he said. "I've lit the fire and put on the kettle, and unpacked the cups. You'll like this house, Em, or I'm a Dutchman!"

Mrs Judkin did like the house. It was a low, grey, stone one standing by itself with a neat garden all round, flowers in front, and vegetables to one side.

"What do you say to the garden, Em?" said Mr Judkin proudly. "Look at all them dahlias! We'll be able to grow all our own vegetables, and there's place for a pig too, *and* a flowerbed up at the station. It's what I've been waiting for all my life."

"It's the smell I can't get over," said Mrs Judkin, drawing in great breaths. "Hay, it must be. Reminds me of when I was a girl. And just think, no neighbours to act nasty."

"Are we always going to be here, Pa?" said Jemima disconsolately.

"And what's wrong with here, may I ask?"

"Well, there don't seem anything but cows and fields and trees. No houses, nothing. Even the railway stops here."

"You don't know when you're lucky, that's your trouble," said her mother, outraged. "You just stop grumbling and count your blessings."

"It's a cup of tea she needs," said her father. "That and a good night's sleep. We'll all feel better after that."

But Jemima did not feel better the next morning. Mrs Judkin was busy unpacking and putting up curtains and losing things and then finding them again. But Jemima was so cross and so little use that her mother said she could get on better without her.

"No more use than a two-year-old you aren't, a-tumbling my crockery around and smashing it. You'd better get out quick before you smash any more. You go into the village and find the butcher and buy some mutton chops for dinner. Best end of neck, enough for three, tell him, and not too fat. You can take a shilling from my purse."

"How do I find the village?" said Jemima sulkily. "I can't see anything but our house and the station."

"You'll just have to go down the lane and ask, won't you? It's no good going up the lane because there's only the station there. Try and be a bit of help and not a hindrance."

At the bottom of the lane was a road, a country road, rutted and dusty. Jemima looked at it disdainfully, and then, seeing a church tower in the distance, shambled off towards it. After ten minutes' walk during which she met nobody but a sheep dog, she arrived in the village. It was nothing more than a huddle of cottages and two or three shops. Nobody was about, except a group of children crouched round some game on the pavement.

"Excuse me," said Jemima officiously, walking through them.

"Who do you think you are?" said one of the boys, blinking up at her.

"My father's stationmaster," said Jemima haughtily.

Nobody seemed impressed. "Last station-master didn't have no children, only pigs," said somebody.

"Perhaps she is a pig, then," giggled another. And this bit of wit so set them off laughing that they were still at it when Jemima came out of the butcher's with her chops.

"It's the dullest, stupidest place I've ever seen in all my born days," she said angrily to her mother when she slammed the chops down on the kitchen table.

"Go and ask your pa what time he wants his dinner," said her mother, "and none of your nasty tempers neither."

Jemima walked on up the lane to the white, wooden fence and pushed open the gate. The station was as quiet and still as the fields and the hills around it. There was no sign of her father, but there was a postman who was con-templating a sack of mail on the platform. It was very different indeed from the hustle and noise of the stations back home. Across the line on a siding in front of the engine shed stood the *Welsh Rabbit*. Smoke plumed lazily

from its tall funnel, and there was a sound of
cheerful voices. There was also a distinct smell
of bloaters.

"I'm Jemima Judkin," said Jemima haughtily to the postman. "Have you seen my pa?"

The postman jerked his thumb up at the
little building with one door and two windows.
"In there with the stationmaster."

"My pa *is* the stationmaster, thank you
very much," said Jemima.

"Mr Davies is till the end of this week,"
said the postman.

Jemima pushed her way into the little room
that seemed to be ticket office, waiting-room
and luggage office all in one. It was cluttered
with parcels and boxes. There was also a table
littered with papers and round this, and con-
sidering a curious machine which had two
dials with letters all round them, were Mr
Davies and her father.

"Yes, well, the telegraph machine, it does
take a bit of knowing, there's no getting away
from that," Mr Davies was saying easily. "I
wouldn't be doing with a new-fangled gadget

like that myself, but the inspector said we ought so's we could get on to the junction at Highchurch if we wanted them urgent. Which I can't say I ever do. And you may be lucky and not get any messages in for a bit."

"But what happens if I do?" said Mr Judkin, agitated.

"Well, you could always send down to the village for me if you was stuck, I daresay. Or there's Master Edward. He knows more about the station than anyone, and he can work that old telegraph machine a treat."

"Who's Master Edward?" asked Jemima.

"Master Edward *Clinton*," said Mr Davies as if this solved everything. "That your girl? No beauty, is she. Still, I suppose she looks healthy, and you must be thankful for small mercies. Well now, we'd best be seeing about getting that milk train off."

"If it's the *Welsh Rabbit* you mean," said Jemima furiously, "they're cooking bloaters on it."

Mr Davies gave her a short look. "Yes, I daresay the *Welsh Rabbit*'s having their breakfast. Fireman wraps the bloaters in wet newspaper and puts them in the fire on his shovel, and when the paper's burnt they're ready and very good too. Very regular in his habits is Mr Pugh. Comes up here nine o'clock or so, cooks a bite of breakfast for himself and Mr Morgan and the guard, and the train's ready to leave about ten."

"But the timetable says the milk train leaves at eight o'clock," said Mr Judkin dubiously.

"Been looking at the timetable, have you?" said Mr Davies. "Ah, none of us pays any attention to that. Never believe what you see in print, that's what I always say. Still, it's rising ten, so we might think about getting her off now."

The *Welsh Rabbit* was standing by the platform by this time, and milk churns were being loaded into the guard's van. At the other end of the train the engine driver and the fireman were in earnest conversation with a passenger.

"Well, Mr Morgan," bellowed Mr Davies. "I'll get her off as soon as you're ready. There's my pig waiting for me down in the village."

The engine driver finished what he was saying, nodded at the passenger, and climbed in a leisurely manner into the cab. The guard gave the last of the milk churns a kick and then walked up with his flag under his arm. Mr Davies walked up to the engine too, and

he and the guard and the engine driver pulled
enormous watches from their pockets and
solemnly scrutinised them.

"Church clock's fast," said the engine
driver. "Don't you go by that, it's not the
clock it used to be. Why, if that isn't Master
Edward coming up the lane. The holidays
must have started. Well I never, Master Edward," he shouted. "Holidays comes round
before you can blink, don't they?"

Heads were poked out of the carriage windows, and the group by the engine swung
round with welcoming smiles.

"Well, Master Edward," said Mr Davies
warmly, "if I wasn't just telling Mr Judkin
here how you knows all the answers about the
station. Master Edward knows it A to Z.
Spends all his holidays up here, and all the
time he isn't at his studies with the Reverend
Williams. You going along with them today?
Jump in then. And if you're going too, missy,
you'd better look quick about it," he added
sharply in a very different tone, to Jemima.

And so Jemima found herself shut into the

carriage with two stout farmers' wives, a mother with a baby in her arms, an old man with a dog on a piece of string—and Edward Clinton.

Everybody there knew Edward Clinton, and seemed to be glad to see him. He sat at his ease, with an arm along the top of the wooden seat. He joked with the farmers' wives, and tickled the ear of the dog who looked at him adoringly. Even the baby, who was too young to speak, jumped up and down on its mother's knee and laughed at him. Everybody was glad to see him—except Jemima. She looked at him disdainfully, decided she didn't like him, and then stared frostily out of the window, hoping that he noticed she was ignoring him.

The *Welsh Rabbit* crept forward in a series of jerks like it had yesterday. And like yesterday, it was just as likely to stop opposite an empty field as by a station. The rest of the passengers did not worry in the least, but went on chattering with gusts of laughter.

"Them heifers of Victor Williams," said one of the stout women, "and he won't mend his hedges. Mr Pugh must be fair wore out chasing them—has to do it every time we come by."

"Ah, Mr Pugh picks up other things than heifers," said her friend. "Something a bit smaller with feathers that he pops into the cooking pot at home. Seen them hanging up in the cab, I have!" And she gave a whoop of laughter, and nudged her neighbours violently with her elbows.

So by the time they arrived at Highchurch junction, Jemima was in a fury. "I come from Bredeworthy. My father is stationmaster there," she said haughtily to the ticket collector, ready to fight him and everybody else if he made a fuss about her having no ticket.

"Come on the *Welsh Rabbit*, have you? Do you know the joke about the *Welsh Rabbit*? One day she was so late that all of us here thought she was the next morning's train come in punctual!" This was obviously a famous joke, and everybody nearby roared with laughter.

"You *are* lucky to live so near the railway,"

said a voice just behind her. It was Edward
Clinton. Jemima tossed her head and walked
away. He could charm babies and dogs and
fat women if he liked; he wasn't going to
charm her.

But she couldn't escape him. Wherever she
walked in Highchurch he seemed to be there,
talking in a familiar way to shopkeepers, and
giving her a friendly nod as she passed. She
soon tired of the town. There was only the
main street and she didn't think much of the
shops. And everybody stood around chattering and talking—you would think there was
no such thing as hurry. It was just like the
Welsh Rabbit all over again.

So back she went to the station, and there
Edward Clinton caught her up again. He came
pattering after her down the station approach
and there was no escaping him.

"If we hurry we'll see the fast London train
to Shrewsbury go through," he said (for all
the world as if he'd known me all my life,
Jemima thought). "That's a Grand Union
one, and they're beautiful trains."

"I happen to come from a place where we saw Grand Union trains every day," said Jemima coldly. "And Hereford and Shrewsburys too," she added. "There was two stations there, big ones—not like *this* place, or Bredeworthy."

Edward Clinton would not be brushed off. "It's a good place for watching trains—Highchurch," he began. But Jemima was not listening. She had got to the bottom of the iron steps that led to the platform where the *Welsh Rabbit* stood. It was still there, but the train was longer, for, between the guard's van and the solitary third class carriage there now stood a truck, and in it, of all extraordinary things, a brougham. No horse, of course, but a brougham with drawn blinds.

Edward Clinton bumped into her as she stood staring and then he let out a squawk of horror. "Corks! That's Grandfather. Quick!"

The *Welsh Rabbit*'s engine was just opposite them, and into this the indignant Jemima found herself being hauled.

"I just don't know what you think you're

about!" she said furiously, trying to wrench herself out of Edward's grasp. There was no room to manoeuvre, either. A step in one direction and she was leaning up against something that might make the train start, and if she stepped back she would fall into the lap of Mr Pugh the fireman who was sitting there on a pile of coal drinking tea out of an enamel mug.

Mr Pugh did not seem in the least surprised. "It's Grandpa, ain't it, Master Edward? Master Edward's grandpa always did throw him into fits. Makes you give over at the knees, don't he? And I can tell you he's in an east windy sort of mood today. Oh yes." Mr Pugh gave a cheerful chuckle and started sucking down his tea again.

"Why've you brought me here then?" said Jemima angrily, trying to find a place to stand where coal didn't crunch under her feet. "There's plenty of empty seats for him and you and me in the proper place for passengers."

Mr Pugh guffawed into his mug. "Sir Lance-

lot Clinton in with all them! That's rich! Sir
Lancelot Clinton's a nob. It's him that's chair-
man of the Grand Union railway (and you've
heard of that, I daresay). And he sits in
Parliament too and makes laws for the country as well as for the railway. Then he comes
down all the way from London without having
to step out of his own private carriage what
took him to the station in London, and makes
laws for Master Edward and his mamma.
Ain't that so, Master Edward?"

"Your grandfather's chairman of the Grand
Union!" said Jemima, forgetting in her
astonishment how cross she was with this boy.
If she had a grandfather who was head of a
railway she'd take care the whole world knew
about it.

"That's it, and as soon as Master Edward
sees his grandpa he bolts for the nearest hidey
hole. Now, here comes Mr Morgan. We'll be
getting the train off early today."

"Well, well, Master Edward," said Mr
Morgan as he pulled himself up into the cab.
"We know why you're here, don't we? Look-

ing to Mr Pugh and me to keep you from grandpa, eh? And my word, the trouble we've had with him while you've been in the town. Getting the truck with his carriage in it off the London train and hitched on to here and him looking out of those windows of his and telling us all what he thought of us."

"I know just what he'd say," said Edward limply.

"Never mind. He goes as sudden-like as he comes," Mr Morgan told him cheerfully. "Here's to hoping he'll be off again tomorrow. And I tell you what, you can take over from me as soon as I get clear of the station."

Whistles blew, steam rushed, wheels ground below them, and the *Welsh Rabbit* moved out of Highchurch. Then Mr Morgan stood aside and Edward squeezed past him and stood in front of all the handles and dials. He seemed to know just what to do. Even Jemima, huddled uneasily on a narrow iron seat, had to admit it, and she wondered however he even managed to stand upright with all the jolting and jarring.

Then came a shriek from Edward, and Jemima saw him wildly pointing. The *Welsh Rabbit* was not moving fast; it had just left some wayside halt, and now it stopped again. Edward jumped down and disappeared.

"Is it his grandfather?" said Jemima, quite concerned.

"Not likely. Master Edward has forgotten about he," said Mr Morgan with a cackle of laughter. "He's after a buzzard's nest."

Jemima could see him now, hauling himself up a tree by the side of the line. She had never seen anybody climb a tree like that, and she watched with grudging admiration. "But won't his grandfather see him?"

"That's Master Edward all over. Never thinks of the consequences," said Mr Morgan placidly. "Well, let's hope his grandpa's taking a little nap."

But events were to prove otherwise. A moment later a resonant voice thundered from the back of the train.

"Edward!" it said with awful meaning.

Chapter 3

THAT VOICE produced dramatic results. Edward looked down, gave a strangled yelp, and slithered to the bottom of the tree in a way that must have taken all the skin off his hands and the knees off his knickerbockers. Then he staggered to his feet and ran wildly to the train. Mr Morgan pulled him in.

"Forgot about grandpa, did you? And there was Mr Pugh and me hoping he'd keep his blinds down and take a little nap behind them. Well, I daresay there'll be a few words at the other end when we get there, eh!" And Mr Morgan gave a guffaw of laughter.

"Will you get a beating then?" Jemima shouted at Edward above all the noise as the train moved off. Edward shook his head but looked utterly woebegone. Jemima shrugged her shoulders. If he wasn't going to be beaten he hadn't much to worry about. Nobody in

Paradise Terrace had ever bothered about anything less than a walloping.

"Here we are, home again," shouted Mr Morgan. "Get ready for the hot water, Master Edward!"

The *Welsh Rabbit* moved slowly into Bredeworthy. Limply Edward climbed down to the platform and Jemima jumped down behind him. For all her boldness she was rather wondering herself what her father was going to say when he saw her, riding inside an engine like this on her very first day.

But her father had his mind on other matters. He was standing in quite a huddle of people. Some were just onlookers, but there were two men in smart green livery, who held between them what seemed to be a short pair of step-ladders.

"Grandfather's men," said Edward dismally. "I wonder when they got here. Nobody even knew when I left home that he was coming down. But he always takes us by surprise like this."

"Why don't you run away if you're so

frightened?" said Jemima scornfully.

"It would make it worse. He's always telling me to be more manly."

The men in livery were fussing with the steps, bringing them up to the truck with the carriage in it. There was a third man dealing with a horsebox behind this, and you could hear the trampling noises and agitated neighing from inside it. A horse was led on to the platform, and at the same time the whole side of the truck beside it was unbolted and carried away, the door of the brougham was opened by a servant, the steps finally pushed into place, and, while the bystanders watched with awe, a majestic figure stepped out and descended to the platform.

Edward's grandfather was very tall and stately. He had a large and stately stomach, an august hooked nose, and a very high and very shiny silk hat. In spite of his size, he stepped down to the platform with kingly dignity and stood looking about him with lofty disdain.

"This train has excelled itself in inefficiency

today," he remarked to the world at large. "I really shall have to write to the shareholders of the Bredeworthy line and tell them that unless they can improve matters on their railway the Grand Union cannot allow them to go on using Highchurch as their terminus. But I regret to say that some of the delay and disorder has been directly caused by my grandson. Edward, don't slink like that, it doesn't become you. Why, may I ask, were you holding the train up just now? And you look as black as a chimney sweep. Have you been riding in the cab?"

Edward shuffled unhappily forward. The servants in livery stared straight in front of them as if they did not hear a word of what was being said, but everybody else was taking a keen interest and looked sympathetically at Edward. "Yes, Grandfather," he blurted, and instantly lowered his eyes to stare at his feet.

"It is certainly against the regulations of the Grand Union that any passengers should ride on the footplate, and I cannot believe that the same does not hold good of the Bredeworthy line. And if it does not, then it should. I suppose that it was you who was responsible for stopping the train to suit your own purposes?"

"It was a buzzard's nest," said the wretched Edward. "I'd seen the buzzard on the fence often before and I thought it had a nest round about there and then suddenly I saw it and then, well..." His voice tailed off into silence.

"Edward," said his grandfather austerely, "you always were a fool. I have not left my boyhood so far behind that I cannot remember birdsnesting. But I do know that I would not have been so childishly stupid as to be caught at it when I knew that trouble would inevitably follow. Why is it you are so different from other boys?"

"I don't know, Grandfather," said Edward weakly.

"You never do know, Edward. That is your great trouble. It is high time that you went to school and learned to be more manly."

The stately figure in its silk hat moved off down the platform. The liveried men now busied themselves with removing the blocks under the wheels of the brougham before it was wheeled down. Sir Lancelot paused by the door of the ticket office and studied Mr Judkin.

"I don't think I have the pleasure of knowing you."

"Judkin, sir, at your service. The new stationmaster as what is taking over from Mr Davies."

"Then I hope matters will improve, at your end of the line at least." Then Sir Lancelot's eye fell on Jemima. "And who, may I ask, is this child? It would seem from her appearance that she has not only been riding on the footplate, but eating her way through all the coal in it as well."

Up till now nothing had defeated Jemima. She had stood her ground with the rudest boys; the Sleepers had been victorious while she led them; she had defied anything that the neighbours could say to her. But Sir Lancelot Clinton with his tall hat and his hooked nose was too much for her. She did not actually run away, but she walked off very fast indeed with her head turned away from her father and the rest of the people on the platform.

"Is that you, Jemima?" called her mother from the kitchen as she came in through the

front door. "Where in the world have you been and me wanting you all this time to put away the china. And lawkamercy me, what *have* you been doing, you naughty girl? I never would have thought that even you could have got yourself in that state."

"I've been at the station," said Jemima defensively.

Her mother gave a screech. "Looking like that? What will everybody think of us, and on your father's first day too! You'll drag us all down, Jemima. Now just you change into a clean pinafore and clean your face and them hands—you'll find a bucket of water in the scullery—and then up you go to the station again and tell your pa his mutton chops are cooked ready and won't wait much longer."

"Have I got to?" said Jemima sulkily. She was not feeling particularly anxious to see her father, after what had happened. "I daresay the mutton chops will keep. Anyway, it's too hot to eat."

"Jemima Judkin! Are you trying to tell me you won't do as you're told? There'll be the wooden spoon about your ears unless you hurry, my girl. Your pa's got to eat his dinner now so's to be back at the station in time to get the afternoon train off. Now you go this very minute and mind you hurry."

But Jemima did not hurry. She splashed in the bucket a bit (but not enough, because she left large grimy smudges all over the towel). Then she took her time about finding a clean pinafore, scowled at her face in the mirror, and, not able to find a comb, ran her fingers through her hair which made it stand out, then smeared them over the top to try to make it lie down. She couldn't find a hat, either, so she did without one. Then she loafed up the lane. She rather hoped she would not meet Sir Lancelot coming down it. It was not that she was frightened of him, of course, but on the whole she thought she would rather not meet him again today.

But the lane was empty. So was the station platform. The carriage and the horse, and the servants in livery had all gone. The *Welsh Rabbit* stood there, but nobody was in it.

There was no sign of her father, but there was the sound of voices in the ticket office. Jemima hesitated, and then went and peeped through the crack by the hinge of the door.

Her father was inside, and so was Mr Morgan the engine driver, who had a mug of tea in his hand and was sprawled in the only chair, talking cheerfully.

"Pity about Sir Lancelot coming just now," he was saying, "because he'll be keeping Master Edward with him up at the White House, and there'll be no one to show you round things with Mr Davies so wrapped up in his pig and his new garden and having no time for up here. And that there telegraph machine takes a bit of knowing. No, I shouldn't worry with all them parcels, they've been there for years and never caused a spot of harm to anyone, and if folks wanted them they'd come and fetch them, stands to reason. But the telegraph machine, that's a different matter. You say it hasn't rung yet?"

"Not in my hearing," said Mr Judkin doubtfully. "But then I was down the platform digging at the flowerbed some of the morning."

"Ah, you're a gardening man," said Mr Morgan happily. "Glad to hear it."

"But what do I do when the bell rings?" asked Mr Judkin. "Mr Davies did start to explain, but then he started off on something else."

"It's a cruel hard thing to learn. I couldn't read them messages coming in. The way that pointer whirrs round the letters then fair makes a man's head fizz." But Mr Morgan sounded very cheerful.

"I'll have to send down to Mr Davies then," said Mr Judkin desperately.

"You'll find it hard getting him from his pig which is in a delicate state on account of her being about to have little ones and being poor at mothering them." Mr Morgan took an enormous swig at his tea. "Now Master Edward, he would be the one for you. Knows everything about the railway does Master Edward, spends all his holidays riding with us and messing about the station. He can work

the telegraph machine a treat. Sends off messages and reads them when they come in. But
there it is, his grandpa's there now, and Sir
Lancelot rules Master Edward and his poor
mamma with a rod of iron—anybody would
be telling you that."

"I'll fetch him and tell him he's needed for
the telegraph," said Jemima through the door.
"And Ma says your mutton chops are ready
and you're to come this minute, Pa."

She didn't wait to hear what was said. She
was off, running down the lane. At least she
had put off the awkward moment when she
would have to give an account of her morning's doings, and hear what her father had to
say about her showing up like a blackamoor
and getting a telling off from the chairman
of the Grand Union railway.

At the bottom of the lane she came across
an old man cutting a hedge, and he told her
where the Clintons lived. It was called the
White House, he said, and Master Edward
had lived there with his mamma ever since
his papa had died. He would have said a lot

more, but Jemima was off. She found the house easily enough, it was not far away, and she strode boldly up the gravel drive which had shrubs on each side of it. There was a big white house at the top with a great many windows. What was to be done now? Jemima stared at the house, and the house stared back.

Then out through the open front door wandered Edward, his shoulders hunched up about his ears, and his chin sunk on to his chest. He stood on the top step, tearing leaves off the creeper that covered the walls.

Jemima now put two fingers in her mouth and whistled the same way as she used to do when she was calling up her Sleepers. It made a really terrifying noise, and she was forbidden to do it. Her outraged mother had often told her that she had never heard of a nicely brought-up child making a nasty, common noise like that—let alone a *girl*.

Edward gave such a start that he nearly fell down the steps.

"Come here," called Jemima. She was not going to call him Master Edward for anybody,

but on the other hand she didn't think she knew him well enough to say Edward.

He looked furtively round him, and then came over.

"What's up?" he asked in a whisper.

"You've got to come and show Pa how to work the telegraph machine," commanded Jemima. "Quick, before that bell starts ringing."

"But there's Grandfather," protested Edward.

"Oh stop nattering on all the time about your grandfather," exploded Jemima. "Why can't you be manly, like what he said."

"Well," hesitated Edward, "perhaps I could come. Grandfather's talking business to Mamma. And he never has lunch, just sherry and a biscuit in his room; it's the only time of the day when he leaves us alone." He looked apprehensively back at the house. "Come on, run!"

"Pa," said Jemima, putting her head round the kitchen door at home a few minutes later. "Here's the boy from the White House who's

come to show you how to work the telegraph.
Only he hasn't got much time."

There was a strong smell of mutton in the
air, and the sound of clattering knives and
forks which stopped suddenly. "JEE mima!"
said her mother. It sounded as if there was
going to be trouble there.

Jemima withdrew quickly. She guessed her
mother knew a great deal more of what had
happened up at the station than she had half
an hour ago, and she didn't feel ready to face
the consequences yet.

"Pa had better come quick. He's got to be
home soon because of his grandfather he
says," she said through the crack in the door.

"JEE *mima*!" said her mother on a higher
and more outraged note.

"Is your name Jemima?" said Edward,
who was standing in the garden among the
broad beans. "What a pretty name."

Now nobody (except her parents of course)
had ever done anything before but tease
Jemima and shout rude things about her
name, and she looked at Edward quite

softened. It had never occurred to her before
that you could actually like a boy; the only
thing she thought they were any use for was
fighting.

And her respect increased when she saw
how he knew his way round the stationmaster's office. He not only could instruct Mr
Judkin on how to handle the telegraph and
how to practise reading messages as the pointer
whirled round pointing to the letters, he knew
his way about all the papers too—and there
were a great quantity of these that had been
bothering Mr Judkin; forms, invoices, notices,
and letters in dingy, dusty piles by the ticket
machine.

"Well, Master Edward," said Mr Judkin
at the end, "it's a pity your grandpa can't see
you now. I'd never have got straightened without you—not being much of a one for paper
work, as you might say."

"You don't really need to do much," Edward assured him. "Mr Davies didn't. Nobody bothers much down here as long as the
milk gets taken off in the morning and the

mail comes. And the cows and sheep and things on market day, of course. Mr Davies just let the station look after itself, and dug the garden and saw to his pigs."

"Well," admitted Mr Judkin, "it's the garden where I want to be..." Then his eye fell on Jemima, who up till now had been lurking behind Edward, but who now had come forward and was investigating the labels on the piles of packages in the corner. "Jemima, just you stop interfering with what ain't none of your business and go home to your ma who's got something to say to you!"

Jemima tossed her head. "*He's* got to go home too," she said. "Come on," she added to Edward.

"Are you frightened of your mother like I am with Grandfather?" Edward asked, as they went down the lane.

"I'm not frightened of nobody," said Jemima violently.

"I bet you would be of Grandfather."

"I would never. I'd stand up to him, that's what I'd do. Bullies have to be stood up to."

Memories of her fighting days surged up in Jemima's mind. "If people creep away from them it makes them worse. You look him square in the face. What's it you're frightened he'll do?"

"I just don't like people being angry with me. Anyway, he's always telling Mamma I ought to go away to school. He calls me a mollycoddle with no spirit in me."

"Show him you've spirit, then."

"How do I do that?'

Jemima considered. "You meet me at the station same time tomorrow and I'll tell you."

Chapter 4

JEMIMA WENT for a long walk that afternoon. After all, though so much had happened, it was only her first day at Bredeworthy and she wanted to find out various things. She had four weeks of holidays; she needed to know what there was to do in Bredeworthy during them, and what the local children were like. She would be starting school with them in September so it was as well to know a bit about them, and whose side she was going to take if there were sides to be taken.

There was also the question of what she was going to say to Edward tomorrow. She had assured him that she would show him how to stand up to his grandfather, so she had better give the matter a little thought.

But after she had stumped through the village—and it was so small that you had passed it and were out on the road that climbed on up the valley before you realised you had been in Bredeworthy at all—she dismissed any hope of the local children. They weren't even worth the trouble of fighting. They sat sprawled outside their cottages and gaped at her and giggled.

However, she did find there was a baker's shop, and as she had threepence in her pocket she went in and bought three penny buns. They were large, fruity, and sticky, and it was while she was licking her fingers after the second bun that the idea came to her. (She always noticed that the best ideas came when you ate.) She and Edward would get Brede-worthy station really smart, punctual and efficient. Her father could tidy up the station garden since that was what he really seemed to like doing, and she and Edward could do the rest. They could see that all the stack of parcels in the ticket office reached the people whose names were on them, they could sort out all the papers by the ticket machine, they could get the trains running to time. That would show Sir Lancelot Clinton that Edward had spirit, and what with him being the chair-man of the Grand Union, he might get so im-pressed with the way the Bredeworthy line was being run that he would let the Grand Union trains run on it, and then it would be a railway you could be proud to belong to.

And at this thought, Jemima, her eyes moist with emotion, licked the sugar from the third bun off her fingers and stood up. Grand Union trains on the Bredeworthy line—that was a challenge!

The next day she was still full of resolution. She was not going to risk that Edward would forget to come. She would fetch him herself, and thereby show that she was afraid of no grandfather, even if he had a handle to his name and a tall silk hat.

She fetched and carried for her mother all that morning, so as to put her in a good mood, and then when dinner-time came she made her announcement.

"I don't want no dinner, Ma." (It was Irish stew, made from the remains of yesterday's best end of neck, and she always hated that, what with the barley and the little bits of bone that you had to spit out.) "But I'll go up to the station and tell Pa his is ready."

"But you didn't eat no dinner yesterday neither," said her mother in a worried voice. "And you being so helpful this morning, it isn't natural. Are you sickening for something?"

"I'm just not hungry, that's all. It's hot, and I like being out of doors this weather."

"It's hot, no mistaking that. Well, you've been such a good girl that I tell you what. I'll put you together a bit of bread and cheese and some bacon, and there's some cold apple pie, and you can take it and eat outdoors."

And so Jemima set out for the White House with a little basket on her arm. She stepped out sturdily, not allowing herself time to linger and be doubtful about what she was doing. Anyway, she probably wouldn't have to see Edward's grandfather, for hadn't Edward said he didn't eat his lunch with the rest of them but sat alone in his room? She would march right up to the front door, pull the bell and demand Edward. After all, they couldn't eat her, could they?

But it turned out she didn't have to pull any front door bell because she came out through the shrubs and saw Edward walking across a lawn by the side of the house. She put her

fingers in her mouth, gave her famous ear-splitting whistle, and walked on.

Too late then she saw what she had done. Edward was not alone. There, sitting under a tree were two more people. There was a lady in a broad-brimmed hat, and there was the august figure of Sir Lancelot Clinton, his high-domed bald head looking as though it had been polished like one of his own Grand Union engines. And both of them had turned round with startled faces and were staring at her, while Edward had stopped dead in his tracks, frozen with horror.

There was no time for hesitation, delay, or apology now. Jemima marched straight up to Edward. "Are you coming?" she said. It was how she would have spoken to one of her own Sleepers, and she didn't see that she need treat him any differently.

"Is this one of your friends, Edward?" said Sir Lancelot, screwing a glass into one eye and frowning through it as he scrutinized her.

"It's the stationmaster's daughter, Grandfather," faltered Edward.

"He said he was coming to the station now," announced Jemima accusingly.

"Is that so, Edward?" said his grandfather.

"Yes, Grandfather, I think I did say something," muttered the wretched Edward.

"Then go. I cannot abide broken appointments and broken promises—however misguided those promises may be."

"I'll tell Cook to keep back some lunch for you, Eddie," called the lady. "I don't know what you can be doing at the station at this time of day, but don't be late home, dear. And try not to get so dirty as you did yesterday."

"Don't mollycoddle the boy, Beatrice," boomed his grandfather. "If he chooses not to be present at luncheon, he must do without it."

"I've got some dinner here," said Jemima as they walked down the drive. "You can have some of it—Ma put in a whole lot."

"But how did you *dare* come?" said Edward. "Walking right up the drive in front of Grandfather—I don't know how you could."

Jemima tossed her head, and suppressed the fact that she had not really meant to do this. "Easy," she said. Then, feeling generous because she found she could almost like this boy, she added, "All you've got to do is not to think about it first. And I tell you, he likes being stood up to."

"Whistling like that!" sighed Edward. "Right under his nose! I tell you what, could you teach me?"

"It takes years and years of practice," said Jemima grandly. "But I'll try to show you, if you like."

And she did show him how to put his fingers in the right position and blow, before she unpacked her mother's basket. They ate the bread and cheese and bacon and apple pie beside a stream that ran through the middle of a field, and Edward, when he had given up puffing hopelessly at his fingers, lay on his front and turned over the stones in the water and looked at the creepy things underneath

them. Jemima unfolded her plans for Bredeworthy station.

"You know," he said at the end. "Grandfather might even get the Grand Union to buy
up the Bredeworthy line. Just think if Grand
Union trains came down to Bredeworthy!
Why, I might even be allowed to drive one!"

Jemima's heart warmed to this boy. "I'd
been thinking things like that," she said.
"Now look, how long have we got to get
things straight? There's a lot we've got to do
in the way of tidying and sorting, which I'm
sure Pa isn't going to do because the engine
driver said not to. Then of course we could
always put on some paint to smarten things
up. But I daresay there wouldn't be time for
that before your grandfather goes."

"You never know when Grandfather will
go," said Edward, who always seemed to sag
when he thought of him. "He comes and goes
so suddenly. Just sends a telegram and comes.
That's how it was yesterday, nobody knew he
was on his way. And he goes like that too. He
might stay all holidays, but Parliament is

still sitting so I don't suppose he will this time."

"You come on up to the station," said Jemima briskly. "I daresay Pa's still having his dinner, or maybe he's digging the flower-bed. At any rate, it isn't time for the afternoon train to go so I expect he's out of the way, and we could have a go at clearing out that ticket office place. I know where he hides the key. And I tell you what, we could go and talk to them on the *Welsh Rabbit* and see if the trains can't be made to run punctual."

But Mr Morgan the engine driver, whom they found sprawled on a folded tarpaulin on the platform, blinking in the sun, was not very hopeful about the *Welsh Rabbit* running to time.

"It's the morning train that throws it all out. The fact of the matter is," said Mr Morgan confidentially, "that none of us—that's me, my mate and the guard—is particular good at waking up. Now my mate, it's him that matters most, as it's him as has to get the *Welsh Rabbit*'s fire agoing and her

steam up. You see, his clock broke a while
ago, so he has to listen for the church clock.
But the church clock being fast he's got into
the way of not paying it the attention he
should. And if the wind's not in the right
direction he don't hear it at all, him being a
heavy sleeper. So there we are, half-past eight
and a damped-down fire to work up (on the
Welsh Rabbit, that is), and breakfast to cook
on it (because me, my mate and the guard
always likes a bite to eat before we begin) so
we're sometimes hard put to it to get her off

by ten, and then the whole day's thrown out. As you know, Master Edward, we've got to take the milk up to the junction by that early train, and bring the mail back midday. That's the train you and your grandpa came on from Highchurch yesterday. Then there's the afternoon up (I'll be taking that off sometime soon) —but of course we've got to have our dinner first—and the evening down—which brought young missy here and her ma down the other day. So you see," said the engine driver triumphantly, "if the wind's wrong and my mate misses the church clock, then we're thrown out for the whole day like."

"But," said Jemima outraged, "it's not ten o'clock the train ought to leave. It's eight o'clock. That's what the timetable says."

"We've never gone by any timetable here," said the engine driver, pulling the cap further over his eyes. "And there never came any good of believing what they say in print. Mr Davies always told us that, and my old father too, and I'll stick to it. Books is all lies, they said."

"It's no good," said Edward, when they had let themselves into the ticket office. "They've never got that train off earlier than ten o'clock in their lives. They'd all have to get up two whole hours earlier—Mr Morgan and Mr Pugh and the guard, and your father too. Oh corks, just look at all this." Edward gave a despondent kick to the boxes, crates and bits of farm machinery that were piled in tangled confusion at one end of the office. "We'll never get it clear."

"Oh stop your moanings, do," said Jemima impatiently. "We won't bother about all this then. We'll see if we can't get them trains running straight—that's what your grandfather notices. See if we can't get him off back to London on a train as is punctual for once."

"And how do we do that?" said Edward listlessly. "You heard what Mr Morgan said. It's impossible. Look, I've got to go. Grandfather will be pacing and raging."

"You stand up to him then. You've got no stuffing," stormed Jemima. "Anybody with

stuffing wouldn't act like you—they'd ...
they'd drive the train themselves!"

"I could drive the train all right," said Edward indignantly.

"Why don't you then?"

"Who'd do the stoking?"

"I would," said Jemima defiantly. "If it's throwing coal through that hole like the thin chap did, I could do that all right."

"But what happens when we get the train to Highchurch?" objected Edward. "They'd see us there sure as eggs, and we'd never be allowed to bring the train back."

"As fast as I think up the answers you go and knock them down," raged Jemima. "I'm not surprised your grandfather says you're such a mollycoddle!"

"What we could do," said Edward slowly, "is get the engine down the line ourselves as far as Mr Morgan and Mr Pugh's cottages. They live just a little way from here and their cottages are right by the railway. So all we'd have to do is stop the train outside and blow the whistle and wake them up. Then they could take over and go on to Highchurch."

"All right," said Jemima decisively. "We'll do that. Tomorrow morning."

"Tomorrow morning!" said Edward appalled.

"What's wrong with that?"

"It's just so soon," stammered Edward.

"Sooner the better. I tell you what I'll do. I'll bang my head six times on the bed knob, wake up at six o'clock, and then come and wake you and we'll both go and start up that old engine."

"Don't you come and wake me," said Edward hastily. "I'll come."

Jemima never knew how banging your head before you went to sleep made you wake at the right time, but it always seemed to work. It did the next morning. She had her mother's old clock that only went tipped forward on its face, and it said ten to six. She pulled herself out of bed and dragged her clothes on, yawning so hard in between that it felt as though her head would fall off. She pulled aside the white curtains over the window and peered out. The sun wasn't up yet, and the hills up the lane were grey and shadowy. But the air smelt fresh and sweet.

She crept downstairs with her boots in her hand, listening to the regular snort and whistle of her father's snoring, and praying that she wouldn't make any noise to interrupt it. She tiptoed across the kitchen and began unbarring the back door. Slowly she wriggled the big bolt and pulled it back, lifted the latch, and walked out into the cool summer morning. She didn't notice that she had no boots on until she felt the icy wet of the grass through her stockings. After the first shock of it she decided that it was as good as paddling, the time she had done it with the Sunday School outing, and she ran on with stockinged feet down the grassy lane to the station.

But of course Edward wasn't there. She might have known he would fail. Well, she would teach him. Even if she had to wake the whole of the White House with her whistling she would bring him out. And she sat down and furiously crammed her boots on over her

soaked stockings and stormed down the lane
again.

She didn't have to whistle. She met Edward
near the gates of his house. He was looking
cheerful and happy.

"I'm sorry you had to get up so early. I
should have told you, we won't be able to go
today. It's market day at Highchurch and
they'll be taking the animals up to the station
to put them on the train. The place will be
stiff with people. We wouldn't have a chance
of getting the engine out without being
noticed. But I thought I'd better tell you."

Never had Jemima been so angry with anybody as she was now. There was a flock of
sheep coming down the road this very minute,
but she cared nothing for them. She stood
there nearly in the ditch while the sheep
surged past with a delicate pattering sound.
The man who followed with his two dogs
stared, but Jemima didn't mind.

"You didn't never want to come," she
stormed. "You're afraid. And you're glad
now you say we can't go. You're fit for noth-

ing but a boarding school—like your grandfather says. Well, I don't care what you're
going to do. I can get on without you. I'm
going to drive that engine myself."

"You can't," said Edward, stung. "Nobody
could by themselves anyway. I tell you I do
want to do it, and I will. But it's no good today, it really isn't. The place is full of sheep
and cattle and people shoving them into
trucks, it's the busiest day of the whole week.
Tomorrow, I promise."

"I'll believe that when I see you," said
Jemima bitterly.

"I'll be there at the engine shed when the
church clock strikes six," asserted Edward.

"Huh!" said Jemima, and turned on her
heel.

Chapter 5

JEMIMA DID not for a moment believe that
Edward would be at the engine shed at six
o'clock next morning, but she went there all
the same. For the second time she pulled on
her clothes before the sun was over the hills,
and stole out of the house up the lane. There
would be words from her mother when she
got back, of course. There had been a fine old
row the day before when she had turned up
round about breakfast time with shoes and
stockings soaked with dew. But Jemima had
never been one to pay much attention to small
matters like that. Besides, she was seething
with righteous anger, and so certain that Edward would fail her that she was rehearsing
already the bitter reproaches she would heap
upon him.

But when she got to the station the white
wicket gate that led off the lane was open. It

did seem that somebody had gone through that morning before her. There was nobody on the platform, and nobody in the ticket office—she peered through the windows; anyway, it was still locked. Perhaps Edward had come and was in the engine shed already. She hesitated, and then jumped down on the railway line. It seemed a very bold thing to do, even though she knew the *Welsh Rabbit* was safely in its shed, and there could be nothing else on the line to knock her down.

One of the big doors of the engine shed was ajar; she paused, and then peered inside. A vast black hulk loomed near her. The *Welsh Rabbit* was huge and frightening when you saw it from this level.

"Edward, are you there?" she called shakily into the shadows.

"Come and help me with the coal," somebody called back.

"Where are you?"

"Up here, of course."

Jemima picked her way down. She felt that a false step would throw her up against the wheels which would roll forward and crush her.

"Come on," said Edward, near at hand now. "I'll help you up.'

The *Welsh Rabbit*, small, cosy even when you saw it standing at a platform in the full light, was a frightening mass of machinery when you were by yourself with it in the shadowy shed, and Jemima found it needed a good deal of nerve to scramble up. Supposing she slipped and fell underneath, among those huge wheels? She stretched at Edward's hand and landed sprawled on all fours on the gritty iron floor.

When she picked herself up she found Edward was stooping with his back to her peering into the *Welsh Rabbit*'s insides. "Mr Pugh always leaves the fire damped down, so we haven't got to light it,

at any rate. But we've got to get it going properly. I've tried to give it a riddle. Now what we need is the blower to get rid of the ash. But of course there's not much pressure."

Jemima was very impressed. She had never seen Edward like this, so calm and confident. It was not just that he was unafraid of the *Welsh Rabbit* (and she had to admit that she was). He seemed to know exactly what to do. She sat down on a heap of coal and tried to brush some of the grit and dust off herself. There was a red glow from the firehole and a faint roaring sound.

"Come on," said Edward. "We need coal."

"What do I get it with?"

"With that shovel of course."

"That a shovel!" said Jemima, peering at the huge implement beside her. "You'd need a whole gang to lift it! And them lumps of coal—they're like boulders. Ma when she starts a fire puts on little nuts of pieces."

"Then we'll have to smash them," said Edward. "There's a pick up there."

So Jemima found herself squatting beside

the coal, hammering and splitting the lumps. She seemed to be doing it for hours and hours, and her forehead dripped with sweat which she wiped off with the back of her hand.

"Cor, your face," she remarked to Edward when he came over for some coal. "Looks like them black minstrels."

"So does yours," he said shortly. "The trouble is I just can't get the pressure up high enough. It's the stoking. Mr Pugh always said it was the trickiest part of all, and I've never done it before. He told me a lot about distributing the fire evenly, but even if I remembered it all I don't think I could do it—the shovel's so heavy and I can't throw the coal back far enough. But you'll have to take over when we start because I'll have to work the controls."

Squatting beside the coal, Jemima watched Edward with some anxiety. He seemed to know his way round all the handles and dials and that, but when was the train going to move? It felt as though they had been there hours already, and she must have hammered a whole coal mine. If they didn't watch out they'd have Mr Morgan and Mr Pugh with them before they had even started, and the train would be as late as ever it was.

Later, much later, when Jemima had hammered mountains more coal and her hands were so raw with blisters that she could hardly hold the pick, Edward straightened up. "I think she's ready now. I'm going to open the shed doors and go out and get the points right. Then we can set off."

Jemima was immensely relieved to see him come back. She didn't care to be left with this hissing, roaring monster, which felt as though it had a life of its own and might take off any minute and run away with her.

"All right," said Edward, hauling himself up. "I'm going to run her back and forwards a bit with the drain cocks open to get water out of the cylinders. Now watch out with that shovel otherwise you'll knock both of us out of the cab. And throw the coal as far back in the firehole as you can and then on each side."

It was terrifying to feel the wheels coming to life and rolling under them. Jemima clutched the side of the cab and watched Edward with frightened eyes. Did he really know what he was doing? Could he bring this monster to a stop if he needed to?

"Come on, stoke!" shouted Edward ferociously.

Stoking was worse than anything Jemima could have imagined. Her hands were now so tender that it was agony to hold anything. It was hard enough to lift the shovel, let alone get any coal on it, and then you had to swing round and throw it in the firehole that was now so hot that she could hardly get near it. But it took her mind off those huge wheels revolving under them. Suddenly they were rolling out into the light. The *Welsh Rabbit* was lurching so that it was hard to keep on her feet.

"Can I stop now?" she panted.

"Stop? We haven't started. We're only just passing the station."

"How much longer?" Jemima felt as

though she was going to fall into the fire, or out of the cab, she was so giddy with exhaustion.

"You mustn't stop. We must keep up the pressure."

Stoop, shovel, turn, throw. Stoop, shovel, turn, throw. Every time Jemima did it she thought it must be the last. Her back, her shoulders and her arms felt as if they had red-hot knives in them; there was a haze with lights dancing in it in front of her eyes. Then a piercing whistle almost threw her to the floor. The *Welsh Rabbit* came to a halt, but continued to whistle. Jemima dropped the shovel and clapped her hands over her ears. She thought they would shiver into bits with the noise.

"It's to get Mr Pugh and Mr Morgan up to the railway," shrieked Edward. "I thought this would wake them up. But they don't seem to be coming. I'll have to go and get them."

By now Jemima was beyond speech. She dimly understood that the *Welsh Rabbit* had stopped, that Edward did not seem to expect any more stoking. In a daze she saw him jump down and disappear. Then she slumped down on to the little iron seat and closed her eyes.

She opened them again when she heard men's voices. Mr Morgan's face was peering up at her from the track. He hauled himself into the cab and stooped to look at the fire and then at all the little clock faces above.

"But what's the company going to say, that's what I want to know! You mean to say you children brought her here—just the two of you?"

"It was quite easy," said Edward's voice from the ground.

"Well, I don't know I'm sure." Mr Morgan pushed his cap back and scratched his head. "I suppose we'll have to be going back to the station to pick up the milk and the passengers now."

Heat and exhaustion had roused Jemima to explosive point. She jumped to her feet. "You just take this train to Highchurch and let it be on time for once. We didn't go through all that for you to be fooling around backwards and forwards between here and the station. Go to Highchurch I say!" she screamed.

"Well I never," said Mr Morgan, staring at Jemima, "proper little spitfire, ain't you. And looking like a blackamoor if ever there was one."

Mr Pugh's head had now appeared. "Take her to Highchurch and pick up the mail," he said decisively. "Otherwise with all this backing and filling we won't be in time for me to get the sausages to take back for the missus for dinner today. Milk will have to wait till the afternoon. Which won't do it no good in this heat, but there it is. Jump down, missy. And tell them at the station where we've gone."

From the track, Edward and Jemima watched the *Welsh Rabbit*, looking very bare without its train behind, trundle into the distance.

Edward gave a long sigh. "If only it could have been a bit farther," he said wistfully. "Or a bit faster. Or a really big train."

"Still, there's tomorrow," said Jemima. Her strength was coming back now. "We'll be quicker another time. Well, I don't know about you, but I'm that hungry I could eat a horse. I'm going home."

"Oh glory," said Edward, feeling his pockets. "I've let them go without their breakfast." He pulled out a collection of flattened, greasy bags and looked at them ruefully. "Oh well, we'd better have it instead."

Jemima's eyes glistened, and she ran her tongue hungrily round her lips. "What did you bring then?"

"I just grabbed what I could find in the larder. I knew Mr Morgan and Mr Pugh didn't like to start until they'd cooked themselves a bit of breakfast. There's some cold sausages and some ham and pie and rolls. I say, you're looking pretty knocked up; sit down and have some."

Jemima was feeling rather knocked up, but half an hour later she felt a great deal better. Her opinion of Edward was also rising. Fancy him thinking of breakfast for Mr Morgan and Mr Pugh. And then he had been so handy with driving the engine. There were other things too. He could talk about climbing trees,

and bird nesting, and snaring rabbits, and
which stream you would find trout in, and
about who went poaching (Mr Pugh, she
gathered, was one). He said he had been
practising the whistle, and that he very nearly
could make the right noise.

Then he scrambled up. "Corks, we'd better
go. It's half-past nine, and they'll be wondering at home where I am, and we told Mr
Morgan we'd go and let your father know
about the *Welsh Rabbit* being gone."

They went back beside the line, which was
uncomfortable walking because of all the
stones. Jemima felt at peace with the world.
She was pleasantly full of food; she and Edward had been very successful with the train,
and she had come to the conclusion that
Bredeworthy was not such a bad place after
all. She would even admit that there might
be more to do here in the holidays than there
had been back home. Seeing her father in the
distance on the station platform she broke
into a trot, as well as she could for the stones.

"*I'll* tell him," she said to Edward. "But,"

she added generously, "I'll say as how it was you who was so clever at the driving. Pa!" she shouted. "The train's gone. It didn't get off at timetable time, but it's earlier than it ever has been, and it's us as did it!"

Mr Judkin was not looking as pleased as Jemima thought he ought. She decided it was because her face was rather dirty. "We got a bit dusty, because of hammering the coal and shoving it on the fire. But I daresay it'll wash off easy enough."

Mr Judkin now found his voice. He said much the same as Mr Morgan had. "You two children *took* that engine!"

"Yes, Pa. Edward drove it, I put the coal on. So's it could be on time for the rest of the day. Only as far as where Mr Morgan and Mr Pugh live and then Edward went and woke them up. We're going to do it tomorrow, only I daresay we can make it a bit earlier then. Soon we'll get it like what the timetable says."

"JEE mima!" exploded Mr Judkin. "You wicked naughty owdacious girl! How I come to have a daughter like you I just don't know!"

"You'll get put in prison for this, I dare-say," said the guard, coming up behind Mr Judkin. "It's against regulations for passengers to ride on the footplate anyway, but what the company'll say to passengers which *drive* the engine I wouldn't like to think."

"We've got the policeman here as it is," said Mr Judkin, who was now in a frenzy of excitement. "Soon as we found there wasn't any engine we sent down to the village for him. And now Sir Lancelot Clinton sending down word that *he* is going off at ten o'clock."

"*Grandfather!*" said Edward, appalled. "Is he going away today?"

"That's what he says. Got to go back to London, he says. Ten o'clock he's coming, he says, and look at us! There's a train all right, and the truck for his carriage, and the horse box, but there's no engine. And the com-motion he made before about the way the line was run. Look, here he is now!"

He was indeed. Jemima could see the carriage in the lane. Even she quailed as that tall silk hat approached.

Mr Judkin hurried to meet him. He was incoherent with agitation. "Begging your pardon—the train has gone—leastways it hasn't but the engine which comes to the same thing for not getting to the junction. And it's all on account of my daughter having driv it off—her and Master Edward. She'll get the biggest walloping she ever had in her life but that won't bring the engine back."

There was a terrifying silence before Sir Lancelot spoke. "You mean to say there is no engine, and that this child and my grandson are to blame?"

"That's what I'm saying, sir," said Mr Judkin.

"And what do you say to this, Edward?"

Edward sagged limply and drooped his head. "We thought we'd try to get the trains running to the timetable," he whispered. "So it meant getting the first train off early, so we took it down to the cottages where the driver and the fireman live so they could take it on to the junction and..."

"Setting aside the outrageous action of taking the engine—you quite forgot that everybody in Bredeworthy now *expects* the first train to leave at ten?"

"Yes, Grandfather." Edward looked as though he was going to collapse with terror.

"It did not occur to you that an engine at Highchurch with nothing behind it was no use to anybody?"

"No," said Edward wildly, "well, that is, we didn't mean..."

"Edward," said his grandfather in a level voice, "you always were a fool but I had not realised quite what a fool you were."

It was here that Jemima sprang into action. She went for Sir Lancelot as she had gone for the Grands back home, but single-handed now. "It's you that is the fool," she shouted at him, "making him so frightened. Anybody can frighten people if they're all dressed up like you with silk hat and all. But *he's* clever, he can drive an engine which is more than you can I daresay for all you tell them how to run the Grand Union." But she had to stop here, gasping for breath.

"JEE mima!" gasped her father, "Oh you owdacious girl just wait ..."

But Sir Lancelot silenced him with a stately gesture. "Well Edward—and notice I address myself to *you* and not to your companion—I have to be in London this afternoon. What do you propose to do about this?"

Jemima dug her nails into her palms until they hurt, and stared at Edward, willing him ferociously to hold up his head and be bold.

For minutes on end Edward stared at his feet. Then he lifted his eyes and looked at his grandfather full in the face. "There's a telegraph machine here. I shall send a message down to the junction and ask them to send a special to fetch you. A Grand Union engine, it would come for *you*."

"Is that all right, Mr Judkin?" said Sir Lancelot.

"That's all right by me if Master Edward can," said Mr Judkin wildly. "He knows its

ways which I can't say I do yet having only just arrived as you might say."

But Edward had gone, and from the ticket office came the clicking of the telegraph machine.

"He seems quite capable," remarked Sir Lancelot after a pause.

"Of course he is," said Jemima furiously. "It's only you as says he isn't. He knows everything about this station and..."

But at this moment Edward came out triumphantly from the ticket office and, in the sight of them all, put two fingers in his mouth and let out a whistle that, as Jemima told him afterwards, nearly sent them all on their faces.

Later, much later, Edward and Jemima sat on a fallen tree and talked it over.

"And you being able to whistle just then," marvelled Jemima. "You had him fair eating out of your hand. I told you he liked being stood up to."

"And he tipped me a whole sovereign." Edward pulled it out of his pocket and looked at it reverently. "And he won't be back for weeks, I daresay."

"It won't matter when he is," said Jemima decisively. "Not now. Look, are you going to show me how to climb that tree for the buzzard's nest?"